THE AMAZING ADVENTURES OF SUPERMAN!

Supergirl's Pet Problem!

by Benjamin Bird

illustrated by Tim Levins

Superman created by Jerry Siegel and Joe Shuster
by special arrangement with the Jerry Siegel family

PICTURE WINDOW BOOKS
a capstone imprint

The Amazing Adventures of Superman
is published by Picture Window Books
a Capstone Imprint
1710 Roe Crest Drive
North Mankato, Minnesota 56003
www.capstonepub.com

STAR34621

Cataloging-in-Publication Data is available at the Library of Congress website.
ISBN: 978-1-4795-6519-1 (library binding)
ISBN: 978-1-4795-6523-8 (paperback)
ISBN: 978-1-4795-8459-8 (eBook)

Summary: When SUPERGIRL finds a strange furry pet, not everything is as it seems.
Soon the tiny creature becomes a massive problem — and the Toyman's to blame! Will
the World's Finest Heroes be able to solve . . . Supergirl's Pet Problem?

Designer: Bob Lentz

Printed in the United States of America in North Mankato, Minnesota.
082015   009140R

TABLE OF CONTENTS

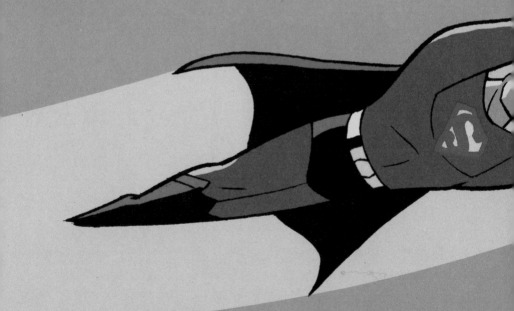

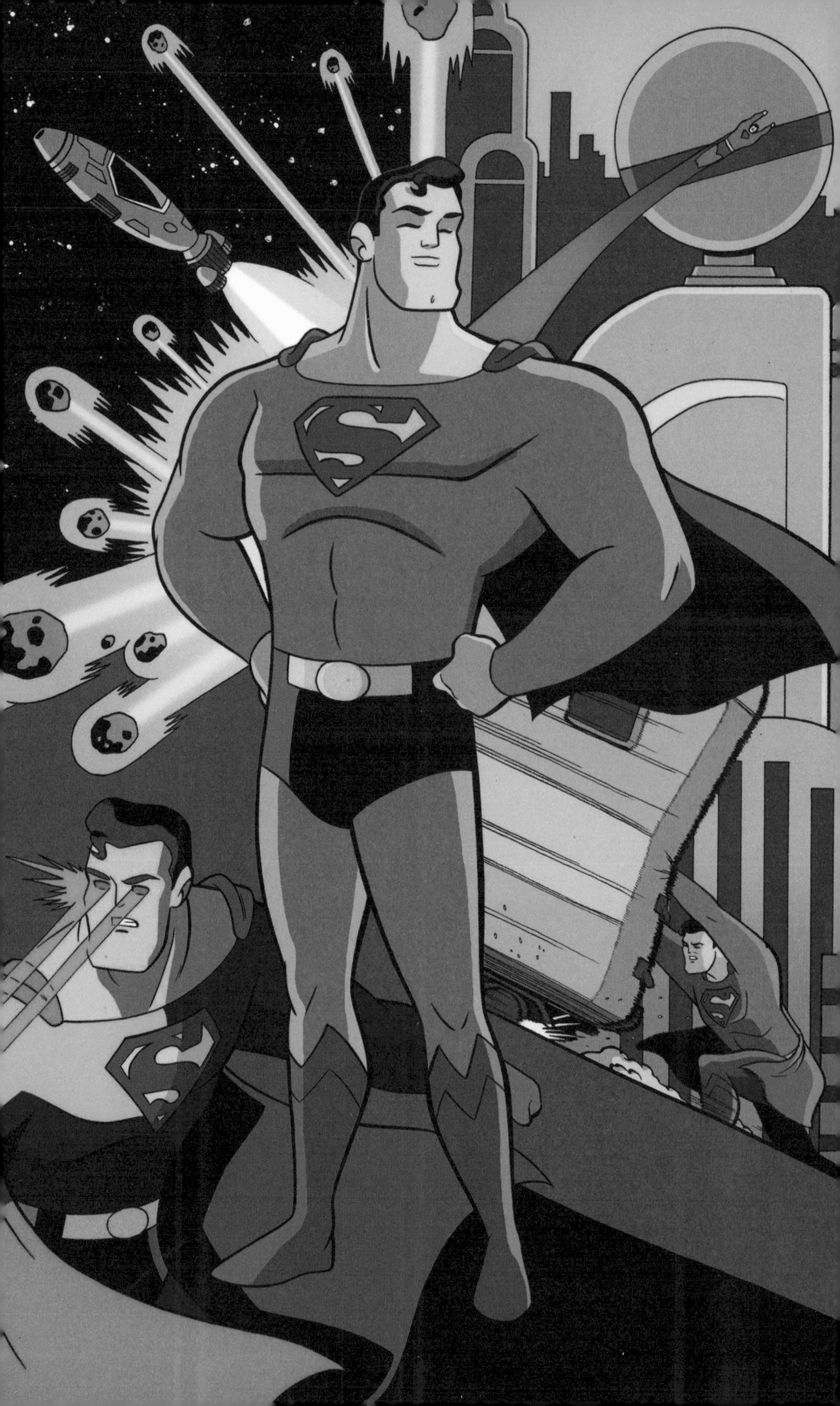

Born among the stars.
Raised on planet Earth.
With incredible powers,
he became the
World's Greatest Super Hero.
These are...

Chapter 1

FURRY FRIEND

FWOOSH!

High above Metropolis, Superman streaks through the clear blue sky. His cousin, Supergirl, soars alongside him.

Supergirl points at the city street below. "Look!" she shouts.

A small, furry animal stands in the middle of busy traffic.

 The super

heroes dive from the sky

like hawks.

Supergirl scoops the tiny

creature into her arms.

The super heroes land
safely on a nearby sidewalk.
Supergirl cuddles the
animal. She strokes its soft,
fluffy fur.

"Eep! Eep!" the creature

chirps with delight.

"Aww, can we keep him?"

Supergirl asks Superman.

"Pets are a big

responsibility," Superman

says. "You have to feed them

and walk them and —"

A fire truck siren

interrupts the Man of Steel.

The fire truck speeds toward a cloud of smoke in the distance.

"I've got this one," Supergirl says. She hands Superman her furry friend.

She rockets into the air.

"What about your new

pet?" Superman calls out.

"I promise to walk him

later!" Supergirl replies and

disappears into the clouds.

Chapter 2
A BIG PROBLEM

Superman grumbles and looks down at the creature in his arms. The tiny furball blinks its little green eyes at the super hero.

"Eep! Eep!" it chirps.

"You're not so bad, are you?" says Superman, patting the creature's head. Supergirl's pet blinks again. When its eyes open, they are glowing red!

The creature starts to shake. The animal instantly grows to twice its size!

"Huh?!" Superman exclaims. He sets the creature on the sidewalk.

A moment later, the creature stands as tall as a nearby streetlight. It towers over the Man of Steel.

"ROAR!" the beast growls.

"Easy, boy," says the super hero calmly.

The beast swings a giant paw at the Man of Steel.

The beast strikes
Superman and sends him
crashing into a nearby
building. **SMAAAAAASH!**
Superman quickly rises
from the rubble.

The super hero takes a deep breath. He prepares to blast the beast with his freeze breath.

The Man of Steel stares at the creature. The giant furball sadly blinks his big red eyes.

Superman holds his breath.

Chapter 3

TOYING AROUND

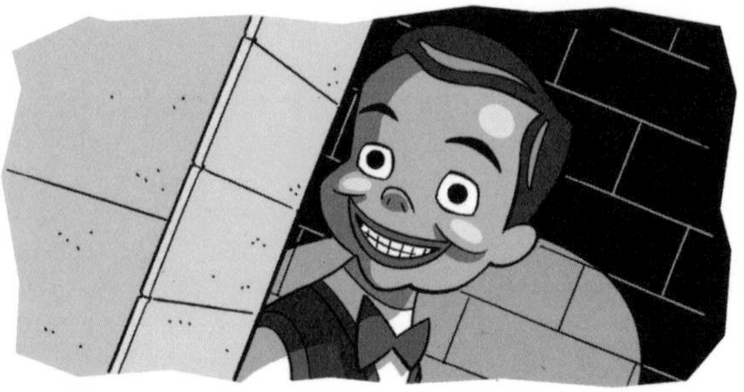

"Tee-hee!" someone laughs.

A tiny man in a blue vest steps out from a nearby alley. He has a wicked grin painted across his face.

The Toyman!

The villain holds a

remote control in his hands.

"I knew Kryptonite

wasn't your only weakness,"

the Toyman

says. "You have

a soft spot for

animals, too."

The Toyman

pushes the joystick forward

on the remote control.

The remote-controlled

creature stomps toward

Superman. Lasers blast

from its red eyes.

Suddenly, Supergirl

returns like a comet.

"It's not nice to toy with people's emotions!" she tells the Toyman.

"Two against one," the villain whines. "No fair!"

The Toyman flees.

Superman finally exhales his freeze breath. WHOOSH! He freezes the Toyman in his tracks.

Supergirl lands and grabs the villain's remote.

"I guess you were right, Superman," Supergirl says. She looks up at the hulking beast. "Pets are a BIG responsibility!"

"And an amazing adventure!" says Superman.

Supergirl pushes the remote's joystick forward. She follows the remote-controlled beast down the sidewalk.

"What are you doing?" Superman asks.

"Just keeping my promise." Supergirl smiles.

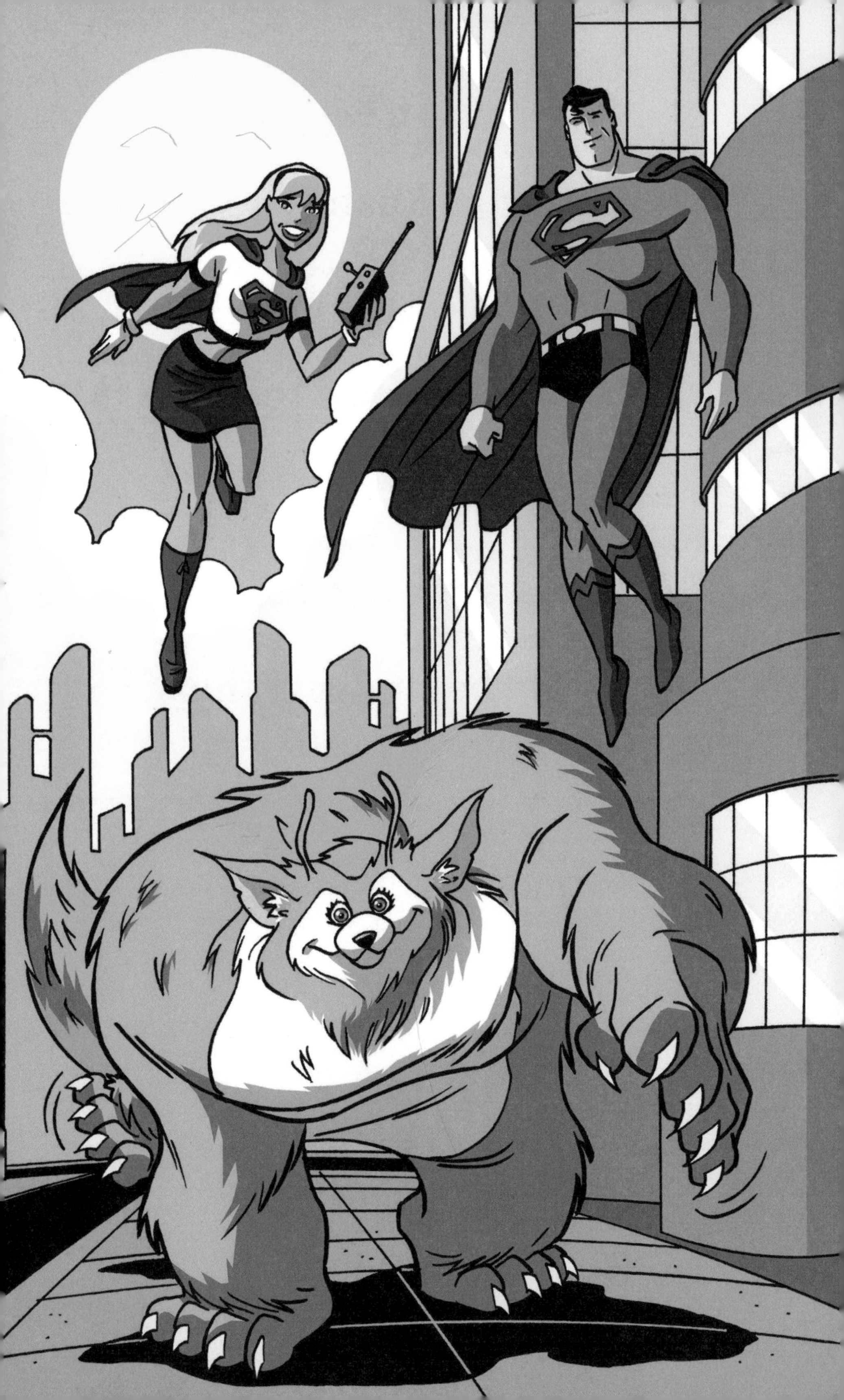

SUPERMAN'S SECRET MESSAGE!

Hey, kids! What's the one thing you need to raise a pet?

Use the code below to solve the secret message!

comet (KOM-it) — an icy space rock that travels around sun in a long, slow path

cousin (KUHZ-uhn) — the child of your uncle or aunt

emotions (i-MOH-shuhnz) — strong feelings, such as happiness or sadness

responsibility (ri-spon-suh-BIL-uh-tee) — having an important duty

rubble (RUHB-uhl) — broken bricks and stones

villain (VIL-uhn) — an evil person

THE AMAZING ADVENTURES OF SUPERMAN!

Battle of the Super Heroes!

Escape from Future World!

Alien Superman!

Creatures from Planet X!

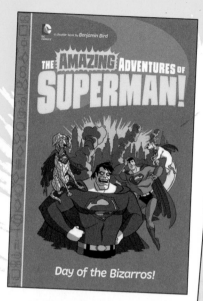

Day of the Bizarros!

Supergirl's Pet Problem!

Bubble Trouble!

Magic Monsters!

COLLECT THEM ALL!

only from . . . PICTURE WINDOW BOOKS

Author

Benjamin Bird is a children's book editor and writer from St. Paul, Minnesota. He has written books about some of today's most popular characters, including Batman, Superman, Wonder Woman, Scooby-Doo, Tom & Jerry, and more.

Illustrator

Tim Levins is best known for his work on the Eisner Award-winning DC Comics series Batman: Gotham Adventures. Tim has illustrated other DC titles, such as Justice League Adventures and Batgirl. He enjoys life in Midland, Ontario, Canada, with his wife, son, dog, and two horses.